SOUL THOUGHTS

A collection of poetry and prose

By: Amzane

Acknowledgments

I would like to thank my family for always supporting me in everything I do. They have been there with me through the good and bad times. Especially my mom for being both my mother and father throughout my life. Without her I wouldn't be the woman I am today.

Many thanks to my lovers and haters for keeping me inspired! This was an amazing journey and I can't wait to continue expressing myself through poetry and prose.

Intro

You are now entering into my most sacred place.
My soul,
Which houses my thoughts.
My thoughts,
Which tells the story of my life.
The story of a girl with lifeless eyes.
It's crazy they say the eyes are the windows to the soul,
But for me that's not the case.
You would never think the girl with the blank, lifeless eyes
actually has the most soul.
My thoughts,
My words,
The inflection in which I speak,
Is the doorway.
The key is here.
Hidden in the words I speak.
I'll need you to listen closely.
My soul is weeping,
Aching to be heard.
On this journey,
You'll reach the door,
You'll hear the cries,
But in order to pass through
And truly hear me.
Truly understand
Why I am the way I am
You'll need to pay close attention
To my Soul Thoughts.

Part 1: Thoughts from a Weeping Soul

"I've always figured thoughts were meant to be hidden. Secrets between you and yourself. Never to be disclosed. Never to exist outside your mind. Never to be spoken through your lips or written down. I've always figured my thoughts wouldn't be understood by anyone. That my thoughts were too outlandish or too weird. I would close my eyes and see words arrange themselves in a way I believed only I could understand. But I've learned that keeping my thoughts to myself did me no good. The words I saw float through my mind, were emotions that I couldn't seem to process. Emotions that I kept hidden deep down that soon made me sick, depressed and unable to truly be me. So I decided to take a leap of faith and disclose my thoughts, my emotions, and my soul."

-- Amzane

"Abandoned"

I was a happy, loving little girl.
Who always smiled and almost never cried.
The apple of my father's eye.
Always dreamed bigger than big.
Found the good in all.
A Pure Soul
That turned into a hateful soul.
No longer did I view the world in white,
But hues of grey and black
The smiles I always adorned became frowns and hateful glares.
Took a turn for the worst.
2006 was the year,
At the age of 10
My world turned dark.
Abandoned by my father,
I vowed to never love.
Could no longer form attachments
For fear of absence.
My heart turned cold!
My mind jaded!

"A Deadly Wish" -- Suicidal Thoughts

Death was once upon a time
A wish
For me
I wanted
Needed
To escape
The pain
That racketed my body
The mental strain
The emotional damage
The scars of abandonment
A child who thought
The only way to escape
Was death
The hurt was so much
I wanted to leave
Didn't care about toys
My thoughts were consumed
By
"If I cut here, will I bleed out?"
Drift into a world
Be held in my grandpa arms
Reunited
With pure love
Fatherly love
Hold his hands
While we walk the roads of heaven
Where I assumed candy grew on trees
But
A voice
My mother's voice
My mother's presence

My mother's love
Saved me

"Hello, it's Me, Depression"

You stare outside and see sunlight but I see darkness. Even in my happy moments, I'm still sad.

Knock Knock
"Who's there?"
"Depression"

Those deadly wishes still enter my mind. I can shut the door, lock it and throw away the key but depression still barges through.

Knock Knock
"Go away! I know what you want!"
Knock Knock!
Knock Knock!

"Hello, its depression, and I just want to wrap my arms around you. Didn't you miss me?"

Feeling of loneliness and despair, slithers through the cracks. Making it easier for those thoughts to come back and ring through.

Knock
Knock
Knock

Depression doesn't just go away.

"Escape"

Escape!
From the pain that tears you down.
Escape!
From the abyss of darkness
That wraps you in coldness
But makes you feel so warm
Escape!
You're only hurting yourself
Stuck in depression
Trapped
Sinking
Quickly
In that slow but quick sand
Escape!
Before you lose yourself
Your strength
Escape!
The mental hold
Fear has you locked in
Can someone help…?
E
S
C
A
P
E

"Disappearing through the Pages"

I don't remember when I read my first book but I do know reading for me started out as homework.

(A little girl with a strict dad who would make her sit down and open up a book. "Read it and then write a summary about the book" is what he would say.)

I don't know if it was the moment he left, or if it was a slow process that happened throughout the years but reading became my escape. I read to connect with characters who had a better life than me. I read to connect with characters that had a worse life than me. I wanted to escape into their world for just a few seconds, a few minutes, a few hours. Reading turned into my escape from reality. My escape from the hurt that I felt deep down inside.

Wait

Am I reading to escape? Or is this just a way to feel some type of connection to my past. A past that was filled with happiness.

*"The words leapt
From the pages
Into her mind
Transforming
The images
That plagued her vision
Into a different state
A state of happiness
Of belonging
She was no longer
Alone
For the words filled
Her soul."*

"Distorted"

Am I alive?
I feel like I'm in a dream
Days passing by like seconds
Seconds going unnoticed
Life flickering
I'm watching from afar
On another planet
A robot with no control
How do I know I'm living
I feel dead
Reality
Fantasy
Synonyms in my world
I have no control
Lost in an abyss
With no escape

"Her

Eyes

Bled

Tears

Of

Sorrow"

"Tears
D
R
I
P
Unto the soil

Her pain
Nourished
That prickly rose
That rose
From grounds
That were thought
To be dead
She gave life
Her hurt
Was not for granted"

"Lucid Dreams"

My life is not a dream but a nightmare that I live daily.
The terrors that plague my mental drives me to a brink of insanity.
Lucid.
Vivid.
Images flashes through and through.
Waking up no longer seems like a solution. I'm stuck in limbo waiting
Waiting
Waiting
Waiting
Enduring
The pain
Hoping
It'll end
But it continues
And I'm tired
So tired
Of sleeping
And living
In a lucid dream
Nightmare

"Tragic Memories"

Tragedy wrote its story in permanent
Marked my thoughts with sadness
Embedded memories in my long term.
Tragedy diagnosed me with depression
Gave me flashbacks
Nightmares
Anxiety
Tragedy drained my aura of its beautiful color
Left me dark and gloomy
Tragedy is me
I have become one with my tragic memories

*"Can you hear my soul crying?
Weeping tears of sadness!
Are you listening?
Are you understanding?
ME!
Why does it feel like I'm screaming my sorrows upon death ears?
I don't understand."*

"Invisible Woman"

No one sees me
But I see everyone
No one sees the hurt
The broken pieces of my spirit
That dull my aura
But I see the smiles that adorn their faces
The happiness that create a celestial glow
That engulfs them in a sense of belonging
I'm alone
In a world filled with billions of people
I have no one
Empty with no way to be complete
I'm trapped
Enclosed by my own thoughts

Part 2: Thoughts from a Damaged Soul

"I feel like my mind has a mind of its own. Thoughts are produced that I would have never thought. Words are said and actions are done without my knowledge. Maybe I'm coexisting. Maybe there's another person in my head that feeds me thoughts when I'm not looking. Speaks for me when I'm silent. Act on my behalf when I'm stuck. Is it possible to blindly coexist? Am I a puppet on a master's string? Or am I just not owning up to my true self? Is it possible that these thoughts, words, actions are mine alone and I'm just scared to admit my true intentions?"

-- Amzane

*"Thoughts best served cold from a cold hearted chick.
With emotions on lock
No key
To access
That hollow dungeon
That is her mind
She dishes it out
The best way she know how
Ice queen
They call her
You should ask about her"*

I go by Amzane
And I love, love
But I also hate love as well
I hate love when love hates me
And I love, love when loves me
But it seems like love hates me more than it loves me
And it kills me inside
To know that I can never truly love, love
Because it will never truly love me
I thought I felt love but the love I thought I felt really hated me
Turned me bitter
Turned me cold
Turned me into an unrecognizable foe
Love broke me
The absence of love
The void from not having someone love me
Broke me
Not having the love of a father
The love of someone important to me
I don't want to be like everyone else
The one with daddy issues
The one who can't trust another man
Because they can't trust their father
Can't love another man because they
Haven't even felt love from their father
I don't want to be a stereotype
A statistic
"Oh yea, you know that black girl over there. Her father left her when she was just ten years old."
The norm
The average
I don't want to continue to grow into a bitter, hateful woman
Who doesn't love, love because all they felt from love is hate

But I'm 23 years old
And looking back, I've noticed
All I was doing was sinking
Lower
And
Lower
Into the bitterness
The hatefulness
That's destroying my soul.

"Under My Skin"

They say hurt people
Hurt people
Well I'm hurt
In an unending cycle
Of pain
Without gain
An unbreakable pattern
A series of forlorn trials
That seem like it'll never end
A permanent frown
Endless tears
Irreversible feelings of despair
That causes me
To inflict
Pain
Suffering
Agony
I'm a torturer
Because I'm tortured
An abuser
Who's been abused
Punishing others
For the hurt done to me

"Unspoken Tears"

Silent
Invisible to the naked eye
My tears are!
Pain
That you'll never see released
My tears are!
Hibernating like a bear for winter
But winter never ends
My tears are!
Weakness
That I never show
Because
I AM
HEARTLESS
EMOTIONLESS
A STONE COLD BITCH
Or so I've been told.

*"I fear commitment
My past told me to."*

"Trust Issues"

Trust doesn't exist in my world.
Humans are selfish by nature,
But you expect me to trust?
Trust my heart with you?
My mind?
My sanity?
Trust is fake
Fantasy
An ideology I don't,
Won't!
Believe in.
Trust is,
Pain,
Heartbreak,
A feeling of despair.
There is no room,
Area,
Crevice,
In my life for
Something called trust.
If me not "trusting" is an issue
Then yes,
I have trust issues.

"No Strings Attached"

I'm not looking for love
Not looking for the
Disappointment
Stress
Hurt
That love offers
I'm looking for pleasure
A mutual agreement
Between two
That begins and ends
With
Satisfaction
I want lust
I want the good
Without the bad
I want you
Only until I release
I don't need you whole
I don't want your heart
But flesh
I crave
Of yours
I have to have.

"Days spent crying
Nights dreaming
Of better
Than I had
I should've been grateful
But my heart
Was empty
My soul was
Yearning
For love
For acceptance
That couldn't be found
Until I found myself"

"Lost Boy"

Lost boy
You left me because you were lost
A boy's mind in a man body
Your father left you
So you left me
But I was your daughter
You were supposed to learn from your father mistakes
Not repeat it
You broke me
But only temporarily

Excerpt from "Jaded Angel" An unreleased song

It all started when I was smaller
Never thought it'd get harder
But I grew up and things changed for the worst.
Let me tell you.
The closest ones were the worst ones.
They turned me into a cold one.
A cold hearted, emotionless, broken-hearted.
Jaded girl.
Hateful girl with jaded eyes.
Eyes that's been blinded by the lies.
Lips that's been silenced by the hurt.
Hurt that only deepened.
So deep I never fully healed.
So deep it scarred the best parts of me. So deep that so far I'm still me.
Jaded.

Part 3: Thoughts from a Healing Soul

"A story that is still being written"

-- *Amzane*

"Fight Back"

As I look behind me, fear begins to creep inside. A shadow, too tall and too large to be mine follows me. "What!?" I gasp, as I try to comprehend what I'm seeing, what I'm feeling. There's no one around but me and I'm beginning to think something unnatural is happening.

Unnatural you say?
No just stupidity!
That shadow represents
The negativity
The hatred
That surrounded you
For years
You've been
Deaf
Blind
But now you
See
Hear
Clearly
The negative forces against you
Ends now!
The fight back
Begins!

"Living for me"

Your burden is not mine to carry
My life is not yours to control
Years
Months
Days
Dedicated to pleasing
You
Hours
Minutes
Seconds
Of me not living for
Me
It's time to break away
From the reigns
You have on me
Free my mind
Let go
Run away
Far
For the grip you've had
Has loosened
The fear I've had
Has lessened
Knowledge gained
Ignorance gone
Your burden is yours
My life is mine

"Meditation"

The turmoil from within
Can only be healed within
Meditating
Begins the healing
Connecting body to spirit
Releasing negative
Accepting positive
Needed to start the process
Of healing
The hurt
The hate
That blackens my inner soul
Slowly
White light fills the lower depths
Each session brings me
Closer and closer
To the goal
I seek
A clean slate where
My past doesn't interfere with my present
Pure energy that
Creates a glow from the inside out
That reaches to all
A connective
Mind, Body, and Soul

*"What is pain but a moment in time?
That eventually ends
Whether it last a minute or a decade
Know that there is always
A rainbow at the end of the storm."*

"A Change in Me"

As I look around me
I notice the change
Around and within me
I've grown
Emotionally
Mentally
Physically
I'm excited for the continued growth
I want to be a better me
I want to strive for the unknown
Achieve a growth beyond my imagination
Love smarter yet harder
Leave my fear behind
Break the barriers
Find my strength inside
But all in all
I want to continue to be me

*"When life no longer feels worth living.
Keep living.
Fight the feeling of defeat
Because there's always a reason to live."*

"To Be"

To be weak
Is to not try
To be strong
Is to give it your all
Never let your weak moments
Overpower your strength
Find yourself
When you feel lost
Be
What others can't
Be
For you

"Naturally Her"

She looks in the mirror
Perfectly imperfect
Her face is chubby
Her hair is kinky
She's not a model
She's natural
Beautiful in her own right
Her stomach pokes out
She's no size 1 nor 6
But she's beautiful and thick
Love her the way she is
Or don't love her at all

"Life
ultimately undeniably yours
The way you live
Will forever be remembered
Death
Is only the beginning
Your essence continues
Forever
Good or Bad
Leave your mark"

"Listen!
There is truth in what I speak
I speak of love, lust, huppiness, and sadness
The four entangled so beautifully
Pure emotions that rages in ways unimaginable
That create the words that flow out of me
In the moment you feel what I feel
See what I see
I pour emotions to the world
So that I'm not alone on this journey called life."

Made in the USA
Columbia, SC
11 July 2021